Dear Parents,

Welcome to the Scholastic Reader series. We have taken over 80 years of experience with teachers, parents, and children and put it into a program that is designed to match your child's interests and skills.

Level 1—Short sentences and stories made up of words kids can sound out using their phonics skills and words that are important to remember.

Level 2—Longer sentences and stories with words kids need to know and new "big" words that they will want to know.

Level 3—From sentences to paragraphs to longer stories, these books have large "chunks" of text and are made up of a rich vocabulary.

Level 4—First chapter books with more words and fewer pictures.

It is important that children learn to read well enough to succeed in school and beyond. Here are ideas for reading this book with your child:

- Look at the book together. Encourage your child to read the title and make a prediction about the story.
- Read the book together. Encourage your child to sound out words when appropriate. When your child struggles, you can help by providing the word.
- Encourage your child to retell the story. This is a great way to check for comprehension.

Scholastic Readers are designed to support your child's efforts to learn how to read at every age and every stage. Enjoy helping your child learn to read and love to read.

—Francie Alexander
Chief Education Officer
Scholastic Education

Ms. Frizzle

Liz

Written by Anne Capeci with consultation by Joanna Cole.

Based on *The Magic School Bus* books written by Joanna Cole and illustrated by Bruce Degen.

The author and editor would like to thank Dr. Wyman Lai, Associate Professor of Pediatrics, Division of Pediatric Cardiology at Mount Sinai School of Medicine, for his expert advice in preparing this manuscript.

Illustrated by Carolyn Bracken.

0-439-68402-1

12 11 10 9 8 7 6 5 4 3 2   5/0 6/0 7/0 8/0 9/0

Designed by Louise Bova.
Printed in the U.S.A.
First printing, January 2005

The Magic School Bus®

Has a Heart

Arnold   Ralphie   Keesha   Phoebe   Carlos   Tim   Wanda   Dorothy Ann

Cartwheel
·B·O·O·K·S·®

SCHOLASTIC INC.

New York   Toronto   London   Auckland   Sydney
Mexico City   New Delhi   Hong Kong   Buenos Aires

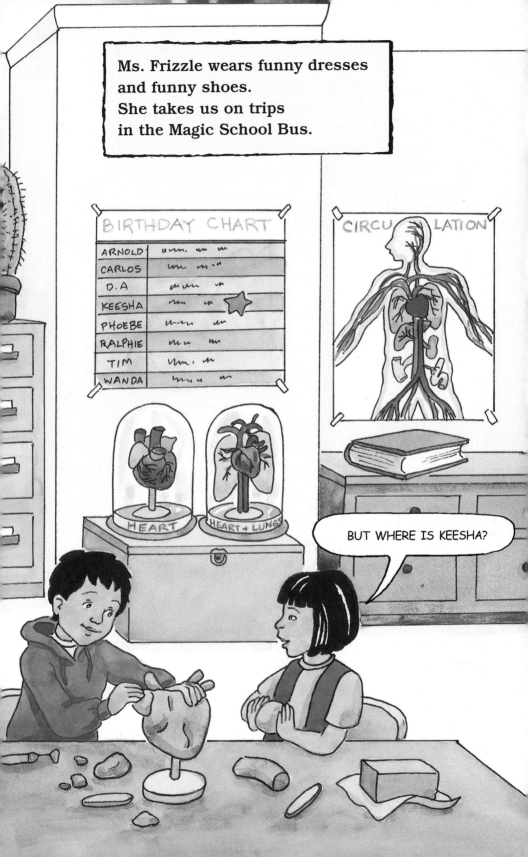

Today is a busy day.
We are going to see a movie about the heart.
Then we will have Keesha's birthday party.

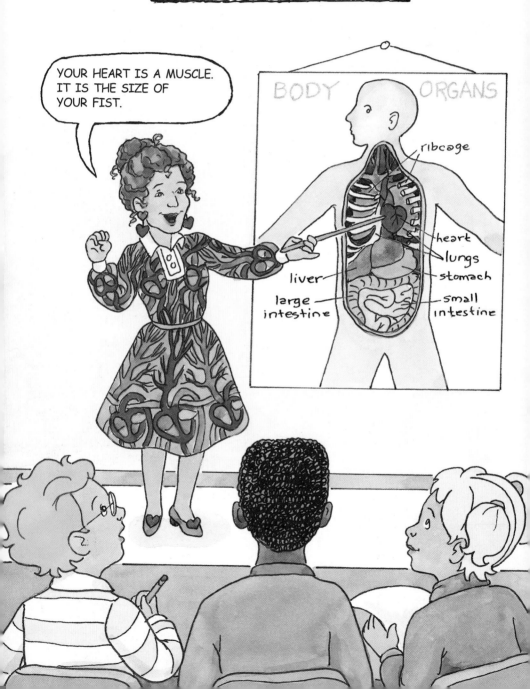

YOU
ARE
HERE

We look out.
The red cells are different.

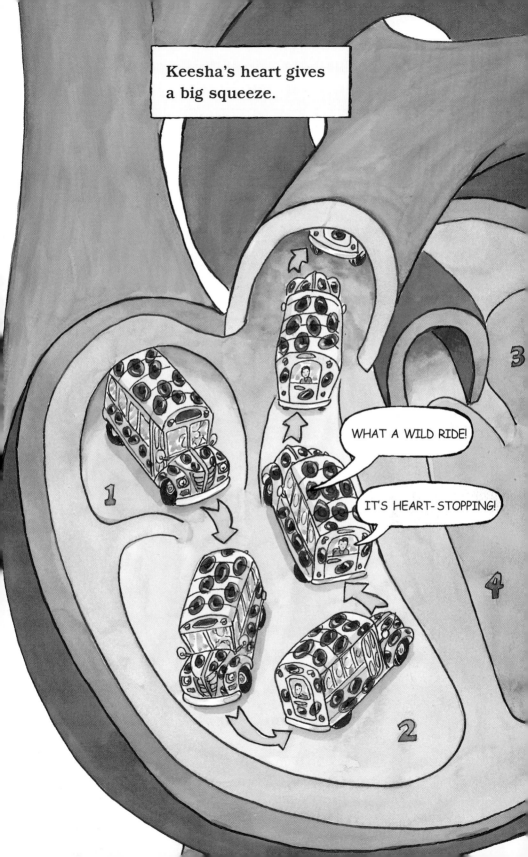

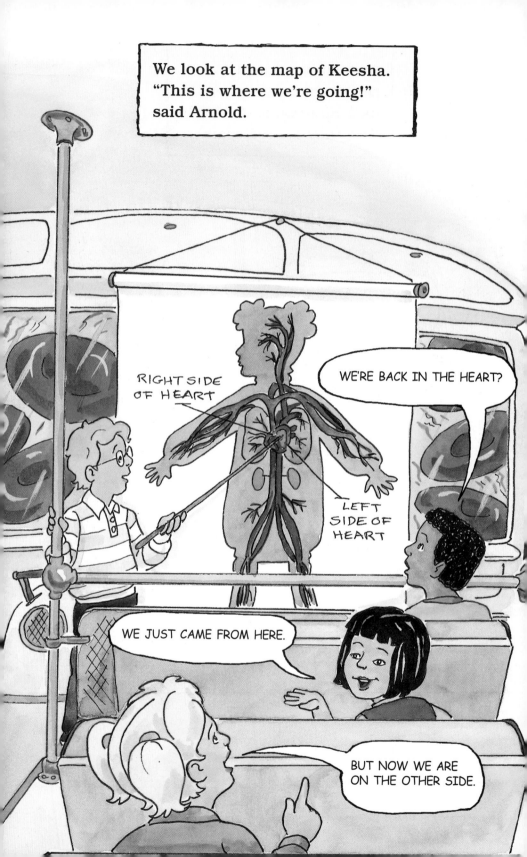

The left side of Keesha's heart pumps us into her body.
We are in the blood vessels again.

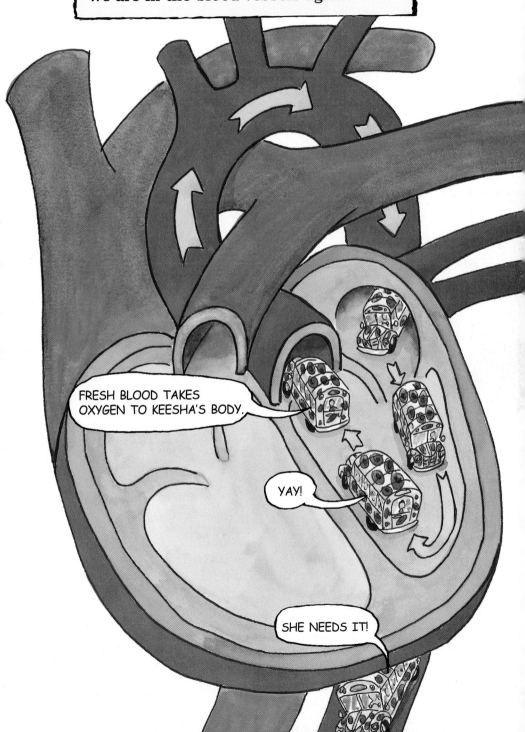

We call to Keesha.
"Now we can all go to the movie,"
said Ms. Frizzle.

MORE ON THE HEART

The heart has four spaces. There are two on the right and two on the left. The right spaces are on the right side of your body. When you look at a picture of someone, it is different. The right side of her heart looks like it is on the left to you. That is why the left spaces of the heart are on the right side of the art in this book.

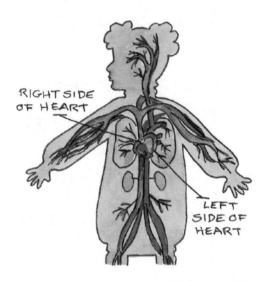

RIGHT SIDE OF HEART

LEFT SIDE OF HEART

HOW FAST DOES YOUR HEART BEAT?

Camel:	30 beats/minute
Person:	70
Lizard:	70
Blue Jay:	165
Mouse:	530
Bat:	750
Hummingbird:	1000